Magic Beans on Toast

by
Derek Keilty

D1643336

Illustrated by Vince Reid

First Published
October 08 in Great Britain by

PUBLISHING

ISBN-10: 1-905637-58-6
ISBN-13: 978-1-905637-58-4

Educational Printing Services Limited
Albion Mill, Water Street, Great Harwood, Blackburn BB6 7QR
Telephone: (01254) 882080   Fax: (01254) 882010
E-mail: enquiries@eprint.co.uk   Website: www.eprint.co.uk

Contents

Magic Beans on Toast

Double Trouble Bubble Bath

Contents

Magic Beans on Toast

Chapter 1
The Climb to Giant Land

'Those beans on toast were really tasty, thanks Gran.'

'You're welcome, Zoe,' Gran smiled, her pointy nose wrinkling. 'I got them on special offer at Wizcos.'

Zoe took her plate over to the sink. 'I'll help you tidy up.' She lifted the bean packet to put it away but as she did, the writing on the packet caught her eye. It read:

Giant Beanstalk Beans
Magic on taste! Magic on toast!
(Warning: Not for planting!)

Tipping one onto her hand, Zoe felt her stomach flutter. *Could a giant beanstalk really grow from such a tiny bean?* she wondered. She slipped the bean into her pocket and when she'd finished helping Gran, she headed for the garden to find out. She didn't tell Gran. Gran would only worry about the warning. Besides, as long as she was careful to plant it where there was lots of room, it would be okay.

In the garage, Zoe found a plastic spade and a watering can. Perfect.

She picked a spot near the bottom of the garden and planted the bean, then gave it a good watering.

She stood back and waited, expecting something to happen - something magic. But it didn't. Then she had an idea how to speed things up. At school, they'd learned how you could feed plants with special plant food to help them grow.

She grabbed her bike. 'Time for a spin to the corner shop.'

She hadn't cycled far, when a loud roar sent her skidding to a stop, almost falling off her bike.

A huge Tyrannosaurus rex came thundering past her, its mouth open and full of dagger sharp teeth.

Luckily, this T-rex was a robot on the back of a truck. A banner fastened to the truck read:

LAND OF THE GIANTS. ANIMATED DINOSAUR EXHIBITION. ALL THIS MONTH AT THE MUSEUM.

It was Mr Fosset from the museum.

'Hi, Zoe,' he called, slowing down. 'What are you up to?'

'I'm going shopping for plant food,' she replied. 'I'm growing a giant beanstalk.'

'A beanstalk - you mean like that one?' he said, pointing at something behind her. Zoe spun round and saw an enormous leafy beanstalk towering in the air.

'Yipeeee! It's started growing,' she gasped. 'I have to go.'

'Don't forget to visit *my* land of the giants,' Mr Fosset called as she sped off, 'and bring your Gran.'

Zoe waved back at him. 'Looks awesome, I won't forget.' But she did. The beanstalk was all she could think about.

By the time she reached the garden it had grown even taller, twisting high into the sky before disappearing through the clouds.

'Gran will go bonkers. I'll have to tell her,' Zoe decided and hurried into the house. But Gran wasn't about. She checked upstairs - no sign.

Racing out to the garden, Zoe stared up the beanstalk as an awful thought struck her.

'Oh no, Gran's climbed the beanstalk,' she cried. 'This is terrible. She could get stuck or fall off and it'd be all my fault.'

Zoe didn't waste a minute. Grabbing a big, leafy branch, she began climbing the beanstalk. It was easier than she thought, almost as if the leaves were lending a helping hand, sweeping her higher and higher. One of her trainers got stuck and she had to leave it behind.

Soon, she was climbing through the clouds. Still there was no sign of Gran. Her arms ached and her stomach churned from being so high. She stopped to catch her breath, then realised she was at the top of the beanstalk. Spreading out in all directions was a lumpy, grey blanket of cloud. She blinked, suddenly noticing that it wasn't cloud at all but land - rocky land stretching for miles in every direction.

'Just like in my Jack and the Beanstalk book!' she gasped.

Immediately, she noticed a path and in the distance, the outline of a castle. It was black with pointy towers and looked a bit spooky but Zoe was sure that's where she'd find Gran.

Arriving at the castle, Zoe sighed. The door handle was much too high for her to reach. She walked round the side of the castle where she spotted a stack of barrels under a high window. Even though her legs ached, she climbed the barrels and peered through the window. She froze in cold terror. Sitting at an enormous wooden table were giants - four of them! They had big, fat noses and wore old-fashioned clothes with big boots. As she stared, to her horror, they all leapt to their feet, clenching their fists, sniffing and snorting. Then, in deep booming voices, they began to chant:

I'm Fee, I'm Fi, I'm Fo, I'm Fum,
We smell a snack for our rumbling tums.
Be they alive or be they dead,
We'll eat their bones with toasted bread!

Chapter 2
Fee, Fi, Fo and Fum

Zoe gasped. The giants were talking about her. These giants were man-eaters, or worse, Gran-eaters!

The fattest, ugliest giant opened a tall cupboard. Hanging inside were rows of scary looking wooden clubs.

'Now what's it to be? How about me Headbludger?' he snarled, running his stubby fingers over the handle of a spiked club, 'or maybe me Clubberumdeblubberclub?' Then, after a pause, he took down a very old club, blowing off the cobwebs. 'No, this calls for Grandpa's old club - the Jackwhacker!'

'When you're ready, Fum, we'll search outside,' ordered a tall, skinny giant, 'Fi and Fo, you two check round the castle.'

Zoe wanted to run away but she could hardly move for fright. And there was Gran too - she had to find her. Her legs trembled, causing the barrels to waver, then wobble then...CRASH! The barrels gave way and she fell into a big, tangly bush.

'Ouch!' she cried, scrabbling around trying not to get spiked by the thorns. The next thing she felt was a huge hand grabbing her arm.

'Gotcha!' growled Fum, wielding the Jackwhacker in one hand and lifting Zoe up into the air with the other.

'Put me down you big oaf!'

He carried Zoe inside to the castle kitchen and called to the others.

The rest of the giants came lumbering in and clustered round her.

'What have you done with my Gran?' Zoe cried.

Sniffing her with his big nose, Fum drooled, 'We likes to eat human beings - we likes to eat human beings on toast!'

Zoe watched horrified as Fi and Fo shoved two enormous slices of bread on the end of spears, then began toasting them in front of a roaring fire. She swallowed a lump in her throat. 'I...I'm not scared of you.'

'Well you should be,' Fum snarled. 'I'm the giantest giant that's ever lived and you better not forgets it!'

'You're not the giantest giant that's ever lived,' Zoe choked crossly, 'dinosaurs are much bigger!'

Fum went into a rage. Face reddening, he smashed the Jackwhacker down on the kitchen table and broke it in two. 'Dinnersaws! Bigger than Fum?' he roared. 'Nothing bigger than Fum!'

'Don't listen to her,' said Fee. 'Humans are always telling lies. Remember what Grandpa used to tell us about the lies Jack told; saying the gold belonged to his pa.'

'Yeah. Anyways, are we gonna talk about stupid dinnersaws or are we gonna have dinner?'

Fum swung his club down towards Zoe's head but Fee caught it at the last moment.

'Hang on a minute,' he sighed. 'Isn't she a bit scrawny?'

Fi brought some toast over. 'You're

right, there's not much meat on her,' he said.

'To feed all four of us,' agreed Fo.

Fum grunted.

'But don't worry,' Fee examined Zoe's skinny arm as an evil grin spread over his face, 'I'll bet there are fatter human beings where she came from.'

Slowly, the rest of the giants nodded, licking their lips. 'There's bound to be - big juicy ones too!' said Fum. 'But how do we get them?'

'You came here by beanstalk, didn't you?' Zoe didn't answer so Fee went on. 'It's the only way humans can visit Giant Land. So you're gonna take us to it. Then we can climb down and eat all the humans we like.'

'No way. I'm not taking you anywhere!' snapped Zoe.

'You need to learn to do what you're told,' growled Fum.

'I won't do anything *you* tell me.'

Fee stroked his long, warty chin. 'Maybe the grats will persuade her!' he sneered. 'Let's throw her in the dungeon - she'll soon change her mind.'

So Fum threw Zoe into a black hole of a dungeon. 'You can rot in there, you little devil!'

16

Chapter 3
In the Dungeon

'Oh bother, where on earth did I put it?'

Down in the garden, Gran had been in the garage the whole time. And she still hadn't found what she was looking for.

'I'm sure I had a bottle of the stuff somewhere.'

She tripped over a pot of paint and fell into a rusty old bath.

Something was digging into her back and reaching round she pulled out a big bottle of green liquid:

Enchanted Weedkiller
Beanstalk strength

She took it out to the garden and poured some all round the bottom of the beanstalk. 'I don't know where you came from but this will sort you out.'

There was a gust of wind, then something bonked her on the head and landed at her feet. She picked it up. It was a trainer - Zoe's trainer.

Gran dashed out to the driveway, almost tripping over Zoe's bike. 'Zoe, are you there?' she called, a lump rising in her throat. She charged round the house calling for her then rushed back outside.

'Bumbling beanstalks,' she gasped, staring up the beanstalk, 'but that means...'

She went into a total panic. Then she realised there was no time for panic. She had to find Zoe and that meant finding her old climbing boots.

* * *

In the smelly dungeon of the giants' castle, Zoe stood banging on the door.

It was quite dark as there was only one candle and sometimes she was sure she could see spooky shadows moving across the walls.

'Let me out of here, you big oafs,' she yelled. She had to escape to find Gran. She couldn't bear to think what the giants might do if Gran stumbled into the castle.

Then she saw something glint in the candlelight. An eye...teeth...big teeth!

As she stared, a horrible looking creature crawled into the light. It was like the biggest ugliest rat she'd ever seen. 'Uh oh, a g...g...grat!' she stuttered, terrified. She reached for a stick of wood lying on the dungeon floor and threw it with all her might but the grat caught it with its teeth, gnawing it to pieces, like a sawmill shredding a log. She backed up, sweat dripping from her nose.

Two more grats appeared. 'Just my luck, there's a whole family of them,' Zoe choked.

White teeth flashed as the grats drew nearer, snarling. It looked like they were about to strike. Zoe closed her eyes - she couldn't bear to look. She heard a noise outside the dungeon door. Had the giants come to cheer on the rotten rodents?

With a loud crash, the door flew open and a long shadow flooded into the dungeon. A figure, too small to be a giant, spun inside the dungeon shaking an enormous bunch of keys. The startled grats scurried away into the gloom.

'Zoe, is that you?'

'Gran! Oh thank goodness,' gasped Zoe. 'But how did you get in?'

Gran held up the keys. 'They might be huge but they're not very smart. They dropped these outside the door.'

Zoe flung her arms around Gran. 'You've seen the giants then,' she sobbed. 'Oh Gran, I'm sorry I planted that silly bean.'

'So that's what happened.' Gran

smiled. 'It's okay, I'm just glad I found you. Oh, I found your trainer too.'

'Then *you* followed *me*. And all the time I thought I was following you.'

'I was in the garage getting some weedkiller to pour on the beanstalk, which reminds me, we haven't much time.'

'You put weedkiller on the beanstalk?'

She nodded. 'Fast acting too. It's probably already started to work.'

They hurried out of the dungeon door and down a narrow corridor.

'What are the giants doing?' Zoe asked.

'They're fast asleep in the kitchen so now's our chance to escape.'

Zoe heard a clucking sound coming from the sack Gran was carrying.

'What's in the sack, Gran?' she asked.

'Oh, it's the cutest little hen,' Gran explained. 'I found it clucking about the castle grounds. Call it a little souvenir.'

Chapter 4
The Giants Give Chase

In the castle kitchen, the giants slept soundly. All except Fee who was staring out of the window at the two figures scurrying away from the castle. A big grin snaked its way across his face and he dug his elbow into Fum's ribcage. 'Geroff,' Fum groaned and rolled over. Fee lifted the Jackwhacker and gave him a whack on the head.

'Ouch,' moaned Fum, sitting up. 'What did you do that for?'

Fee pointed out of the window. 'Look.'

'Wha...but how'd she escape?' Fum felt for the keys on his belt and realised they were missing. 'Me keys, the little worm has stolen me keys. C'mon, let's get after them.'

'Not so fast.' Fee held him back. 'And she didn't steal your keys. I let her go!'

'Let her go! You gone nuts or something? Now we'll never find the beanstalk and gets to eat fat, tasty humans.'

'Oh stop whining. It's all part of my brilliant plan.' Fee gave Fi and Fo a kick. 'I figured that that Gran human the girl kept babbling on about would turn up eventually, so I planted the keys in the dungeon where she'd find them. Now all we have to do is follow them back to the beanstalk. Honestly, I don't know what you'd all do without me sometimes.'

Fi and Fo got up, rubbing the sleep from their eyes. 'What's going on?'

'We'll explain on the way,' said Fee. 'Now c'mon, they're headed down by Cloudy Gaps. And keep your big fat heads down.'

* * *

Zoe and Gran soon reached the beanstalk which had turned a browny-yellow colour.

'Looks like the weedkiller's started to work,' gasped Gran.

'Is it safe?'

'We'll be fine, it usually takes a while to work.'

They were halfway down when the beanstalk began to shake madly.

Even though it had started getting dark, Zoe peered up the beanstalk and saw the soles of feet - giant feet!

'It's the giants!' she cried, 'they must've followed us and they're climbing down the beanstalk. Look!'

'I don't have to - I can feel them.'

In her panic, Gran lost her footing and fell, tumbling down the beanstalk, only just managing to grab hold of a branch as she fell. Zoe scrambled down and helped her get a foothold on the beanstalk.

Next thing, they heard one of the giant's voices boom, 'Hurry up you lot or we'll all end up like Grandpa!'

At last, Gran and Zoe clambered down the last few metres to the garden.

Gran fetched an axe from the garage and swung it at the base of the dying beanstalk. But she swung it so hard that the blade got stuck. Zoe grabbed the handle and they both pulled, only to see Fum's huge foot swing down from the branch above their heads and kick the axe halfway across the garden. He leapt off the beanstalk, landing in the garden with a thud. There were three more thuds as the other giants landed beside him.

Zoe swallowed a lump in her throat as all four giants circled them.

'Think you could outsmart a giant, did you?' Fee sneered.

Fi rubbed his stomach. 'All that climbing has made me hungry...'

'Starving,' added Fo.

'...for human beings on toast,' roared Fum. 'So let's go raid some human castles!'

'You're a rotten lot, you giants,' Gran fumed.

Fee laughed. 'And you've got rotten luck and guess what - it's just run out. So, maybe we'll start by eating you!'

Fum's outburst about castles had given Zoe an idea. The museum down the road used to be a castle and she remembered about Mr Fosset's Dino display.

'You don't wanna waste time eating us,' Zoe blurted out. 'Wouldn't you rather start with the biggest, fattest humans first?'

Gran looked at her as if she'd gone bonkers, till Zoe winked at her.

'Of course,' growled Fum.

'Then follow us, we can show you. Grab your bike, Gran.'

Fum shook his fist in her face. 'There's no escape y'know...so don't try anything stupid.'

Chapter 5
Attack of the Dinosaurs!

Zoe and Gran cycled down the road
with the giants lumbering after them.

Cycling round the corner, Zoe pointed
to the big stone pillars at the entrance to
the museum and yelled, 'There! That's where
all the big, tasty humans live!'

The museum was locked up for the
night but Fum easily kicked open the door.

The giants stormed inside, not noticing Zoe and Gran darting under their legs.

All around there loomed the tall, dark shapes of the animated dinosaur exhibition. Gran crept alongside Zoe past a big T-rex. 'I take it you've got some sort of plan?'

Grabbing Gran by the hand, Zoe dashed behind the main desk of the reception area and flung open a cupboard. 'Quick, we've got to find the control panel that operates the dinosaurs.'

Gran opened another cupboard exposing a panel with lots of buttons.

'That's got to be it,' gasped Zoe.

'But which one do we press?'

'Any of them...all of them.'

They both began pushing buttons till, with a loud roar, a huge T-rex sprang to life. Then, beside it, a fierce triceratops stomped forwards from some big fern bushes and began thrashing its three-horned head from side to side. Soon all around them a host of prehistoric reptiles sprang to life among the fake ferns and trees.

The dinos were very realistic but just to make sure, Zoe only kept a few lights on. 'I hope the giants haven't heard that dinosaurs are extinct.'

By the looks on the giants' faces, Zoe was sure they hadn't. The four giants froze, the blood draining from their cheeks.

Fum threw his arms in the air. 'It's a trap!'

The T-rex opened its mouth exposing rows of dagger-sharp teeth. Zoe knew it was a robot but even she felt a shiver.

'Told you you weren't the giantest giant that's ever lived,' she yelled at Fum.

The rest of the giants backed up towards the door but Fum swung a fist at the T-rex then screamed with pain, yelling, 'Stupid dinnersaw's got skin as hard as a club.'

'Oh and did I mention what they like most to eat? Yup - giants!'

For the first time Zoe was sure she spotted the giants tremble.

Gran was fast becoming an expert at the controls and had all the dinos on full power; the roar was deafening.

'You'd better go back up the beanstalk,' yelled Zoe above the din, 'or they'll be after you and they won't stop till they've eaten you.'

As the T-rex lurched forward Fee cried, 'Run lads!'

Zoe followed them out to make sure they headed back towards Gran's house and the beanstalk but to her horror she felt herself being scooped up by a giant hand, the breath nearly squeezed out of her.

'You think you're so smart,' Fum growled, his cheeks reddening with rage. 'Well you've gone too far this time. And maybe if I eat you I won't feel so bad.'

Fum licked his lips and was about to make a snack of Zoe when there was a loud roar and another T-rex appeared charging along a nearby street, travelling very fast. Zoe blinked, then realised that it was Mr Fosset's truck. Fum kicking in the museum door must've triggered an alarm at Mr Fosset's house, she guessed.

Using her last ounce of strength, Zoe found enough breath to wheeze. 'There's no escape, they can smell you!'

Fum gasped, watching the giant T-rex speeding along; the truck was hidden from view by a hedge and it looked as if the

T-rex was running. Zoe thought she couldn't have planned it better herself.

The giants were thrown into a mad panic. 'They're all over the place!' said Fee.

Fi screamed. 'That does it! I'm getting out of here!'

'Yeah, me too,' said Fo. 'We came here to find food, not *be* food for dinnersaws!'

Fum dropped Zoe and stomped after them. 'You're not leaving me to fight them all.'

This time, the giants did stomp off down the road back to Gran's garden. Zoe and Gran followed from a safe distance on their bikes. Moments later, Zoe pointed to the dark shapes scurrying up the beanstalk.

'The giants are climbing back up. Look!'

'We did it!' Gran cried.

Arriving at the garden, Gran and Zoe stared up the beanstalk as the last pair of giant heels disappeared into the night sky.

Then they both let out a huge cheer.

Gran lifted the axe but had only just taken aim when the ground trembled under their feet. It was like an earthquake.

They both fell down as the beanstalk was ripped out of the ground, showering them with soil, its long, snaky roots ascending into the starry sky.

'The giants, they've pulled up the beanstalk from Giant Land,' panted Gran.

'Looks like they're making sure in case dinos can climb.'

And moments later, the giants and the beanstalk were gone.

The next day, Gran threw out all of her packets of magic beans.

Then they went to the museum to make sure everything was okay.

As soon as they turned the corner they walked straight into the back of a long queue of people.

A smiling Mr Fossett came hurrying over. 'Bit of a break-in last night,' he said. 'There's a rumour going round that the culprits were giants, four of them too. Wouldn't be anything to do with your beanstalk, Zoe?'

Zoe shook her head. 'Er, couldn't have been. My beanstalk withered away.'

'Don't look so worried, I'm over the moon. Business has never been better. In fact, I'd like you to have these two free tickets for the exhibition.'

Zoe and Gran had a great time at the museum and when they got home, Gran made boiled eggs on toast.

'Best if you don't mention our little adventure to Mum and Dad,' said Gran, 'you know how they worry.'

Zoe nodded. 'I'm glad you didn't make beans on toast,' she said, tapping her egg with a spoon. 'I don't think I want to see another bean for a very long time.'

Zoe tried to cut the top off her egg but couldn't. A piece of shell broke off and she stared, wide-eyed at what lay underneath.

'Gran, this egg wouldn't happen to have been laid by that hen you took from Giant Land, would it?'

'Yes, I collected it this morning. Is it okay?'

Picking off the rest of the shell, Zoe set it back on her egg cup and watched it gleam in the sunlight from the kitchen window - a beautiful, shiny, golden egg.

Double Trouble Bubble Bath

Chapter 1
Gran's Amazing Bathtub

Zoe flew upstairs to the bathroom.

'Wow!' she gasped, staring at her Gran's new bathtub. It was enormous, bright green and shaped like a clover leaf.

Zoe had begun pulling off her shoes and socks when Gran came in. 'Can I try it, Gran?'

Gran smiled. 'Course you can.'

Gran helped her fill the bath with warm water then turned a silver knob on the side of the bath. The water bubbled noisily.

'Awesome!' shrieked Zoe.

Gran cackled, her pointy nose wrinkling. She handed Zoe a yellow plastic duck. 'Have fun!'

Zoe was about to get in when she paused.

'Bubble bath?' She searched around the bathroom but couldn't find any. She opened a cupboard under the sink. Inside, there were rows and rows of colourful bottles. She read some of the labels, gasping. They all had the weirdest names.

Things like Spider-Toad Conditioner and
Batwing Body Spray. Zoe stayed at Gran's all
the time but she'd never noticed them
before. She spotted a dusty green bottle
called Double Trouble Bubble Bath, then
smiled. It looked a bit old but bubble bath
didn't go out of date, did it? She poured
some into the bath. Soon the bath was full
of bubbles. Zoe put Duck in, then got in too.

'Everything all right?' she heard Gran
call.

'Great thanks, Gran.'

Then something odd happened. Zoe suddenly noticed that there was another yellow duck floating next to the one Gran had given her. Exactly the same - except it had a strange little cross face. 'Where did you come from?' she said aloud.

The next thing she heard was someone snigger behind her. Her heart thumped against her ribcage. She spun round and stared into her own freckly face. Zoe thought she was looking into a mirror - but there was no mirror and the little girl was real. Zoe shot out of the bath.

'Who are you?' gasped Zoe.

'Who are you?' her twin shot back rudely.

'I'm Zoe.'

'I'm Ozy.'

'But that's impossible, you're me.'

'I'm not you, I'm me. Anyway, leave me alone', Ozy turned on the tap.

'You're filling the bath too full,' Zoe cried.

But Ozy just laughed, splashing Zoe in the face. 'Don't be an old spoilsport.' She smacked the water with her hands, shrieking.

Zoe wiped the bubbles from her face.

'Gran's floor's getting soaked.'

'Who cares about Gran's floor?' Ozy scowled. 'Get out of the bathroom! You've had your turn.'

Zoe gasped, 'Are you always so nasty?'

She heard Gran's voice calling from downstairs. 'Zoe, what are you doing, there's water dripping from the ceiling?'

'It's not me,' Zoe protested.

Next thing, the bathroom door burst open. It was Gran - she didn't look very happy. 'What's going on? Who were you talking to?'

'It wasn't me, it was...,' Zoe's voice trailed off as she realised her double had vanished into thin air!

Chapter 2
The Trouble Doubles

Gran sighed. 'I know you've been having fun but try not to wet the floor.'

'Sorry, I'll mop it up, Gran,' Zoe apologised.

As Gran left, Zoe heard a giggle. A big bubble floated in front of her face. Zoe gasped. Staring out of the bubble was Ozy's face, grinning among the rainbow colours.

The bubble floated lower over the bath water, then... Zap! Ozy suddenly reappeared with a big splash.

She grabbed the yellow duck and threw it at Zoe. 'Neyaaaa! Dive bomber ducky!' It bonked Zoe on the head. Ozy began fiddling with the silver knob on the side of the bath. She turned it round and round. The bath bubbled faster and faster. Then she pulled it off.

'You've broken it!' cried Zoe. 'And I'll get the blame.'

'Yippee! Least now no one can turn it off.'

'I've had enough of this!'

Zoe stormed into her bedroom to get dressed. After a while, she couldn't hear any noise coming from the bathroom and began to wonder if she'd imagined it all.

She checked the bathroom. No sign. Then she heard Gran calling her for lunch.

'Did you enjoy your bath?' Gran asked as they tucked into some tasty beans on toast.

'It's mega, Gran. Sorry about the floor.'

After lunch, Zoe went back upstairs to her room. Opening the door, the colour drained from her cheeks. 'Oh no, look at the place!'

Her bedroom looked like it'd been

struck by a tornado. Toys and games littered the floor, and clothes and bedclothes were scattered everywhere.

Then suddenly...THWACK! Zoe got a pillow in the face.

'C'mon, let's have a pillow fight,' shrieked Ozy. The pillowcase ripped open and feathers flew everywhere, filling the room.

'I thought you'd gone,' cried Zoe, lifting her Barbie. Its head was hanging off. 'You've broken this?'

'S'only a stupid doll,' scoffed the double.

'And look at this room. Gran will go bonkers!'

'Are you always such a borey, snorey, goody goody? Let Gran tidy it, isn't that what Grans are for?' the double snickered, ripping another pillow. 'Yippee, it's snowing!'

'You're going to tidy it!' said Zoe firmly, 'before I get the blame.'

'Not likely! Tidying up is boring, I'm off!' And before Zoe could stop her, Ozy shot out the door. Zoe tried to follow her but couldn't open the bedroom door. Ozy had locked her in her room.

'Let me out!' Zoe cried. But Ozy just laughed.

Zoe slumped on the bed. Ozy was totally impossible. How was she going to get rid of her? How was she going to get out of her room? She had an idea. Sliding a piece of card under the door she poked a pen into the lock, pushing out the key. The key dropped onto the card and she slid it back under the door.

On the landing, she heard water splashing from the bathroom. A lump rose in her throat. She opened the bathroom door and gasped.

In the bath sat not one look-alike but two....

Chapter 3
Panic at the Pool!

'If you won't play with her - I will!' snapped the new double. And they both began throwing face cloths and squirting toothpaste at each other, laughing hysterically.

'Who are you?'

'If you must know, I'm Yoz.'

'Not another double,' gasped Zoe.

'Can't you just play normally?'

'It's you who's not normal,' sneered Ozy. 'We're not doing anything wrong.'

'Then how come you have to hide in a bubble when Gran comes and magic your own nasty friends to play with you?'

Zoe decided there was only one thing to do. She ran downstairs and told Gran to come quick.

Gran rushed upstairs to the bathroom.

'Awesome bath, Gran,' the doubles chorused. The floor was like a swimming pool.

Gran lifted the bottle of Double Trouble Bubble Bath, frowning. 'Oh dear.'

'What is it?' asked Zoe.

Gran pointed to the sell-by date on the bottom of the bottle. 'I'm afraid this bubble bath's a hundred years out of date. It says use by 31st October 1908. The ingredients have all gone off!'

Zoe glowered at the doubles. 'So have those two!'

Gran said, 'Well, I know what I'm going to do with this.' And she began pouring it down the sink.

The doubles both looked horrified. 'You can't do that!' shrieked one of them. 'Yeah, we might want to make more doubles!' cried the other. And in a flash they both turned into bubbles.

Zoe seized her chance. She poked one of the bubbles with her finger. Pop! It burst and Yoz vanished. 'Quick Gran, pop the other one,' Zoe cried.

But Ozy was too quick. She reappeared, snatching the bottle off Gran. Then, grabbing a towel, she raced into the bedroom.

Speeding after her, Zoe tried the door handle. 'She's locked it again.'

'I've a spare key in my room!' said Gran.

When they got inside, however, they were in for a shock. The window was open and Ozy was gone.

* * *

Gran had started the car and called for Zoe to hurry up when she heard her cry, 'My bike's missing. She's taken my bike!'

They set off in hot pursuit. 'What on earth's she up to?'

'Trouble,' said Gran. 'It's what she's made of.'

'I can see her. She's up ahead. She's turning into...'

'The swimming pool,' Gran finished.

The pool was very busy and Gran took longer than she'd have liked finding a parking spot.

Zoe and Gran hurried into the spectator area just as Ozy came out of the changing area wearing Zoe's pink bathing suit. She walked towards the packed pool holding the Double Trouble Bubble Bath and smiling smugly.

Zoe suddenly realised what she was up to and gasped. 'We've got to stop her; she's going to put the bubble bath into the pool.

Then there'll be a whole pool full of trouble doubles!'

Zoe climbed over the railing of the spectator area.

'Give me that bottle.'

'Not likely, I'm going to have fun with this.' Ozy unscrewed the lid, laughing madly. 'Time to fill the whole town with doubles... the whole world!'

Zoe lunged at her but Ozy was too quick.

Suddenly, a whistle blew. 'Oi, no spectators in the pool area,' shouted a cross-looking pool attendant.

Zoe cornered Ozy.

Zap! To escape, Ozy turned into a bubble. But as she did, she dropped the Double Trouble Bubble Bath, which rolled slowly towards the edge of the pool.

'Zoe,' Gran cried, 'the bubble bath!'

Zoe spun round. She was about to make a dive for it when a big hand grabbed her shoulder. 'I told you, you're not allowed near the pool.' It was the pool attendant. Zoe watched in horror as the bottle rolled towards the edge of the pool, closer... closer...closer...

Chapter 4
The Double in Deep Water

The pool attendant turned to look at the bottle and Zoe shrugged him off, diving for the bottle, only just grabbing it before it fell into the water.

'I got it Gran...Gran?' Zoe couldn't see Gran anywhere.

Then a voice cried, 'I'm up here!'

Zoe gasped. Gran was standing on the

top diving board. Everyone in the pool stared at her. The bubble was floating higher, past the diving boards towards the top board. And Gran was waiting, clutching a hairpin. 'Can you see the bubble, Zoe?' Gran called.

Zoe squinted and could just make out the bubble, floating past the middle diving board. 'Yes, you'll see it any second.'

69

The attendant was blowing his whistle furiously. His cheeks were so red and puffy, he looked like he was about to explode.

The bubble floated higher, higher, then...pop! Bull's eye! The bubble and the double disappeared.

'Hurray!' cheered Zoe.

The bewildered pool attendant helped Gran back down the steps of the diving board.

'Have you two gone mad?' he puffed. 'You'll have to leave or go and get your swimming costumes before I get the sack.'

Gran turned to Zoe. 'Fancy a swim?'

Zoe did. But first Gran had to take

her to buy a new swimming costume as her old one had disappeared with the double.

They had a great swim and afterwards Gran took Zoe for an ice cream.

'Gran, what are all those strange bottles under your sink?' Zoe asked, curiously.

'Best if we keep them, and today's adventure, our little secret.' Gran winked as they queued for their ice cream.

Zoe nodded. 'I don't think Mum or Dad would believe me anyway.'

The man at the ice cream counter held up his scoop. 'Now ladies, double chocolate or vanilla?'

Gran and Zoe both laughed. 'Definitely vanilla!'

Also available in the Reluctant Reader Series from:

PUBLISHING

Alien Teeth   *(Humorous Science Fiction)*
Ian MacDonald   ISBN 978 1 905637 32 2

Eyeball Soup   *(Science Fiction)*
Ian MacDonald   ISBN 978 1 904904 59 5

Chip McGraw   *(Cowboy Mystery)*
Ian MacDonald   ISBN 978 1 905637 08 9

Close Call   *(Mystery - Interest age 12+)*
Sandra Glover   ISBN 978 1 905 637 07 2

Beastly Things in the Barn   *(Humorous)*
Sandra Glover   ISBN 978 1 904904 96 0
www.sandraglover.co.uk

Cracking Up   *(Humorous)*
Sandra Glover   ISBN 978 1 904904 86 1

Deadline   *(Adventure)*
Sandra Glover   ISBN 978 1 904904 30 4

The Crash   *(Mystery)*
Sandra Glover   ISBN 978 1 905637 29 4

The Owlers   *(Adventure)*
Stephanie Baudet   ISBN 978 1 904904 87 8

Snakes' Legs and Cows' Eggs   *(Multicultural)*
Adam Bushnell   ISBN 978 1 905637 21 8

57

A Marrow Escape *(Adventure)*
Stephanie Baudet   ISBN 1 900818 82 5

The One That Got Away *(Humorous)*
Stephanie Baudet   ISBN 1 900818 87 6

The Haunted Windmill *(Mystery)*
Margaret Nash   ISBN 978 1 904904 22 9

Friday the Thirteenth *(Humorous)*
David Webb   ISBN 978 1 905637 37 9

Trevor's Trousers *(Humorous)*
David Webb   ISBN 978 1 904904 19

The Library Ghost *(Mystery)*
David Webb   ISBN 978 1 904374 66

Dinosaur Day *(Adventure)*
David Webb   ISBN 978 1 904374 67 1

Laura's Game *(Football)*
David Webb   ISBN 1 900818 61 2

Grandma's Teeth *(Humorous)*
David Webb   ISBN 978 1 905637 20 1

The Bears Bite Back *(Humorous)*
Derek Keilty   ISBN 978 1 905637 36 2

The Gladiator's Ghost *(Historical)*
David Webb   ISBN 978 1 905637 59 1

The Alien Science Bus *(Sci-Fi)*
Derek Keilty   ISBN 978 1 905637 46 1

Order online @ **www.eprint.co.uk**